DISNEY·PIXAR
MONSTERS, INC.

Sulley Visits the DOCTOR

By Melissa Lagonegro

Illustrated by Atelier Philippe Harchy

A Random House PICTUREBACK® Book

Random House 🏠 New York

Copyright © 2004, 2014 Disney•Pixar. All rights reserved. Published in the United States by Random House Children's Books, a division of Random House, Inc., 1745 Broadway, New York, NY 10019, and in Canada by Random House of Canada Limited, Toronto, in conjunction with Disney Enterprises, Inc. Pictureback, Random House, and the Random House colophon are registered trademarks of Random House, Inc. Originally published in slightly different form as *Monsters Get Scared of Doctors, Too* by Random House Children's Books in 2004.

ISBN 978-0-7364-3127-9
randomhouse.com/kids
MANUFACTURED IN CHINA
10 9 8 7 6 5 4 3 2 1

"Achooooo!" Sulley wasn't having a good day. He was home sick with a bad cold.

"Sulley, you're one big furry ball of germs!" exclaimed Mike. "You need a doctor!"

But Sulley didn't like going to the doctor. He wanted to get better on his own.

The next day, Sulley went to work. But his stuffy nose and aching head made it really hard to get his job done.

As the day went on, Sulley's cold got worse and worse.
"Sulley, if you blow your nose any more, it might fall
off," said Mike. "A doctor can help you!"
But Sulley wouldn't go to see one.

That night, Mike tried to make Sulley feel better.
"You need a hot bowl of Mama Wazowski's
homemade stinkin' soup," said Mike. "And a doctor!"

"Please, Mike, no doctors," replied Sulley. "I'm scared of what they might do to me. I'll be alone in a strange room—and what if it HURTS?"

"You won't be alone, pal. I'll be with you," said Mike. "And the doctor will tell you everything she's going to do before she does it."

Mike explained all the things that would happen during the exam.

Sulley felt less frightened after listening to Mike and finally agreed to see the doctor.

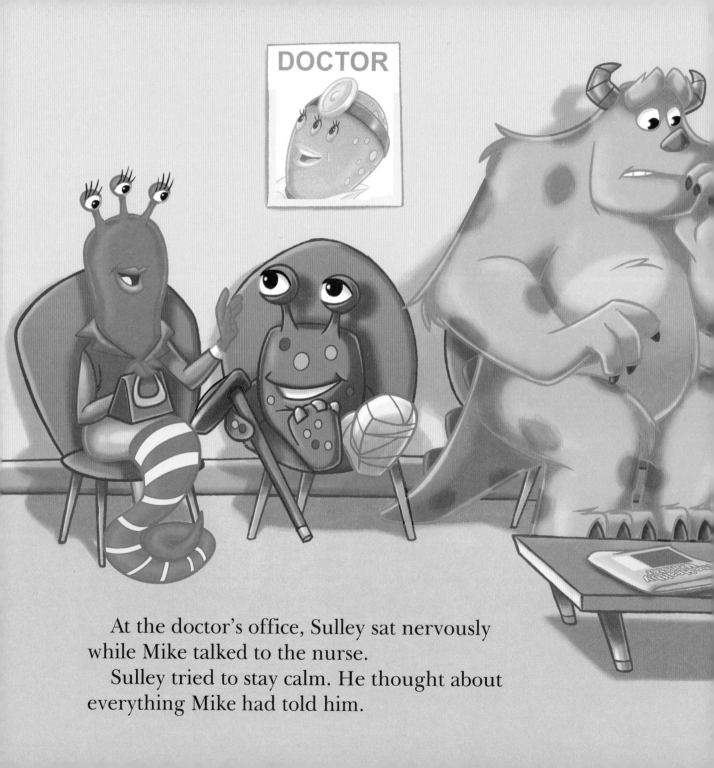

At the doctor's office, Sulley sat nervously while Mike talked to the nurse.
Sulley tried to stay calm. He thought about everything Mike had told him.

"Mr. Sullivan, the doctor will see you now," said the nurse with a smile.

"Nice to meet you, Sulley," said the doctor.
She talked to Sulley for a while and made sure he knew everything that would happen—just as Mike had said.

She took Sulley's temperature, looked in his ears and throat,

listened to his heart, and checked his blood pressure and reflexes.

"You were a great patient!" said the doctor. "Now drink lots of fluids and get some rest!"

"That's it?" asked Sulley. "It's over?"
"See, pal?" said Mike. "There was nothing to be afraid of."

A week later, Sulley was feeling a lot better.

"Glad to see you back in the swing of things, boss," said Mike.

"I couldn't have done it without you," replied Sulley. "Now, if only we could get you to go to the dentist!"

DON'T RUN IF YOU'RE SCARED—
STAY CALM.

DON'T YELL AND DON'T TEASE.
DON'T MAKE EYE CONTACT.

ASK THE OWNER BEFORE PATTING A DOG.
ALWAYS PAT ITS BACK, NOT ITS FACE.

LET AN UNFAMILIAR DOG
SNIFF YOUR HAND.

"Remember, Mike, even though dogs slobber, have big teeth, and make loud noises, that doesn't mean they're scary. We have a lot of loud, slobbering friends—just think of Ricky."

Back at work, Sulley took Mike into a kid's room where there was a nice, quiet dog.

"Stay calm and let him sniff me," remembered Mike. "I am funny, I'm not scared, and dogs are my friends."

Before long, Mike was telling jokes and collecting laughs. He was slowly getting over his fear of dogs.

Thanks to Sulley's help, Mike became the top Laugh Collector again—and he even grew to like dogs.

"Maybe *I'll* get a dog," declared Mike.

"Maybe you should start with a hamster," said Sulley with a chuckle.

Sulley taught Mike all about dogs and gave him tons of safety tips. Together they read stories and watched videos about friendly dogs.

"Don't worry, pal," began Sulley. "I'll show you some things to do when you're around dogs—and maybe you won't get as scared next time."

At home after work, Sulley talked to Mike about his fear.
"I'm scared to work when I feel like a giant chew toy,"
cried Mike.

Inside, Mike tried to tell a joke—but he was so nervous that he just froze with fear.

"Nice d-doggy, good d-doggy," stuttered Mike.

Suddenly, Sulley realized that Mike was afraid of dogs!

Sulley noticed that Mike didn't want
to go into the kid's room. So he snuck
in behind him to find out why.

"What are you waiting for, buddy?" asked Sulley. "There are kids to crack up and laughs to collect."

"I . . . uh . . . d-dropped my contact lens," said Mike.

"That's a good one, funny man," Sulley said as he pushed Mike toward the door. "The kids will love your new material."

Mike really didn't want to face another dog. So he needed a good excuse.

"I can say I have monster pox, or . . ."

But just then, Sulley arrived on the laugh floor.

". . . DOG!" Mike had a problem—he was terrified
of dogs!

"I can't make the kids laugh when there's a dog
around," thought Mike. "Those drooling fur-bags
think I'm a big rubber ball!"

It was business as usual at the new Monsters, Inc., where monsters collected laughs from human kids to use as energy.

Mike Wazowski was one of the top Laugh Collectors. But lately, he was having trouble on the job.

"Oh no, not again!" groaned Mike as he read the paperwork for his next assignment. "This kid has a . . ."

DISNEY·PIXAR

MONSTERS, INC.

PUPPY PROBLEMS!

By Melissa Lagonegro
Illustrated by Atelier Philippe Harchy

A Random House PICTUREBACK® Book

Random House 🏠 **New York**

ISBN 978-0-7364-3127-9
randomhouse.com/kids
MANUFACTURED IN CHINA
10 9 8 7 6 5 4 3 2 1